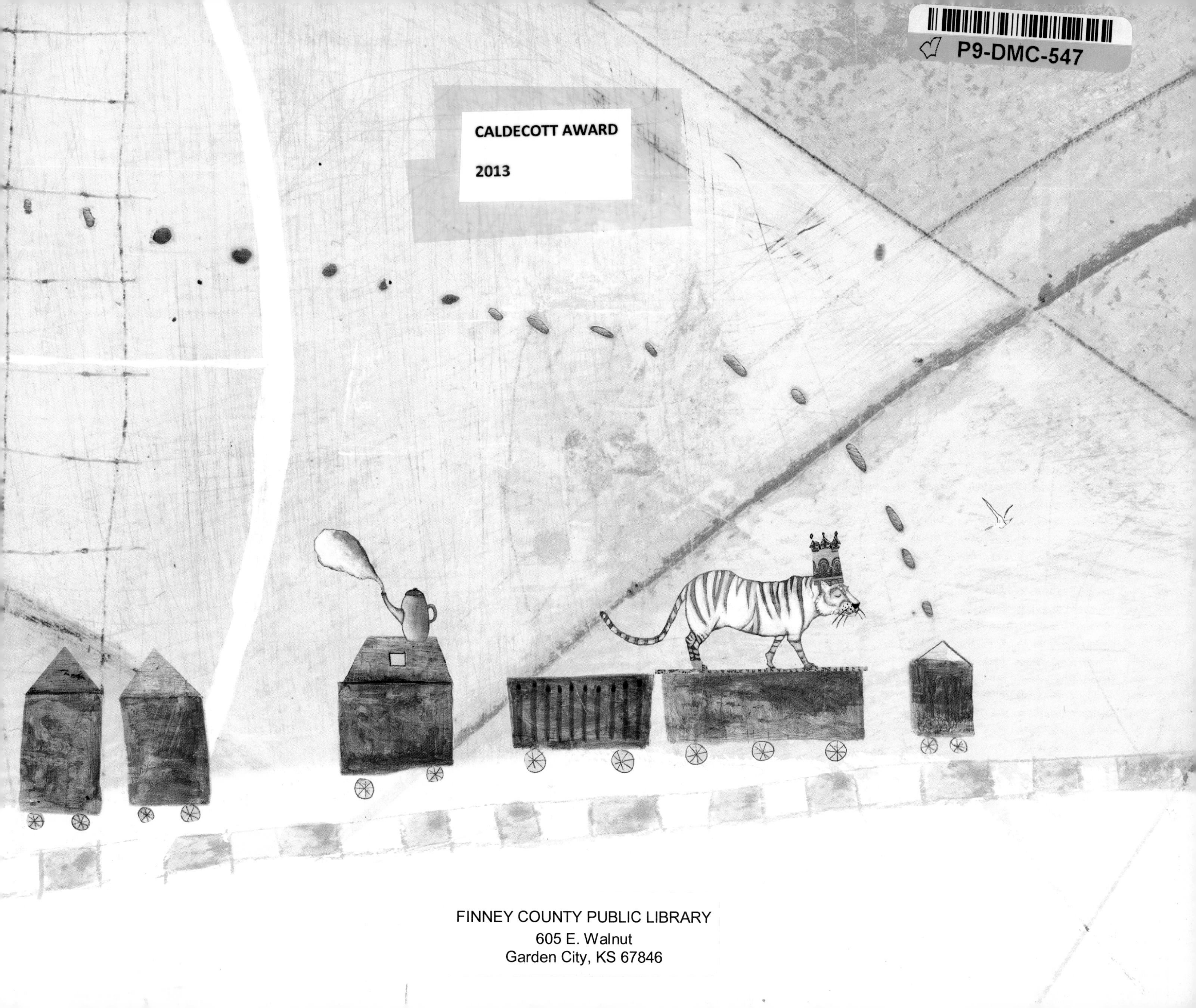
CALDECOTT AWARD
2013

For my niece Juliet, who never wanted to go to sleep.
— M.L.

For my mom and dad, and for the fewer than four thousand tigers that exist in the wild today.
— P.Z.

Houghton Mifflin Books for Children is an imprint of Houghton Mifflin Harcourt Publishing Company.

www.hmhbooks.com

The text of this book is set in Bembo.
The illustrations are mixed media paintings on wood, and computer illustration.

Library of Congress Cataloging-in-Publication Data is on file.
ISBN 978-0-547-64102-7

Manufactured in the U.S.A.
WOZ 10 9 8 7 6 5 4
4500405588

Sleep Like a Tiger

written by Mary Logue
illustrated by Pamela Zagarenski

Houghton Mifflin Books for Children
Houghton Mifflin Harcourt
Boston New York

Once there was
a little girl
who didn't want
to go to sleep
even though
the sun had
gone away.

ENTER HERE

She told her mother, “I’m not tired.”

She told her father, “I’m just not sleepy.”

They nodded their heads
and said she didn't have
to go to sleep.
But she had to put
her pajamas on.

She picked out her favorite pajamas
that matched the night sky.
“I’m still wide awake,” she announced.

Her parents said that was fine.
But she should wash her face and brush her teeth.
So she did. It felt good to be nice and clean.

Then, because she loved
climbing into her bed,
she did, stretching her toes
down under the crisp sheets,
lying as still as an otter
floating in a stream.

"Does everything in the world go to sleep?" she asked.

"Yes," her parents told her.
"Our dog is sleeping right now,
curled up in a ball on the couch,
where he's not supposed to be."

"And the cat is fast asleep,
stretched out in front of the fireplace,
the warmest spot in the house."

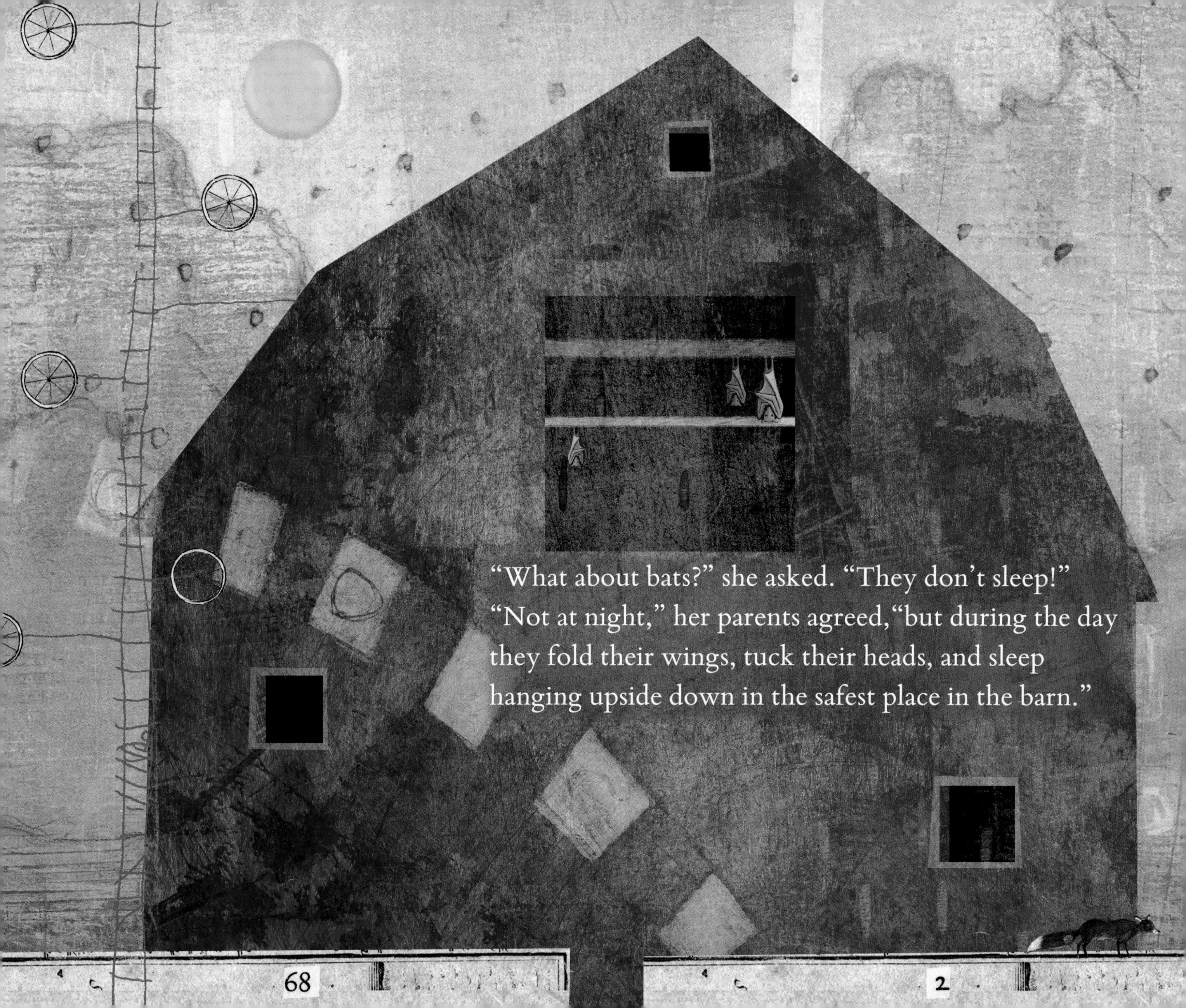

"What about bats?" she asked. "They don't sleep!"
"Not at night," her parents agreed,"but during the day they fold their wings, tuck their heads, and sleep hanging upside down in the safest place in the barn."

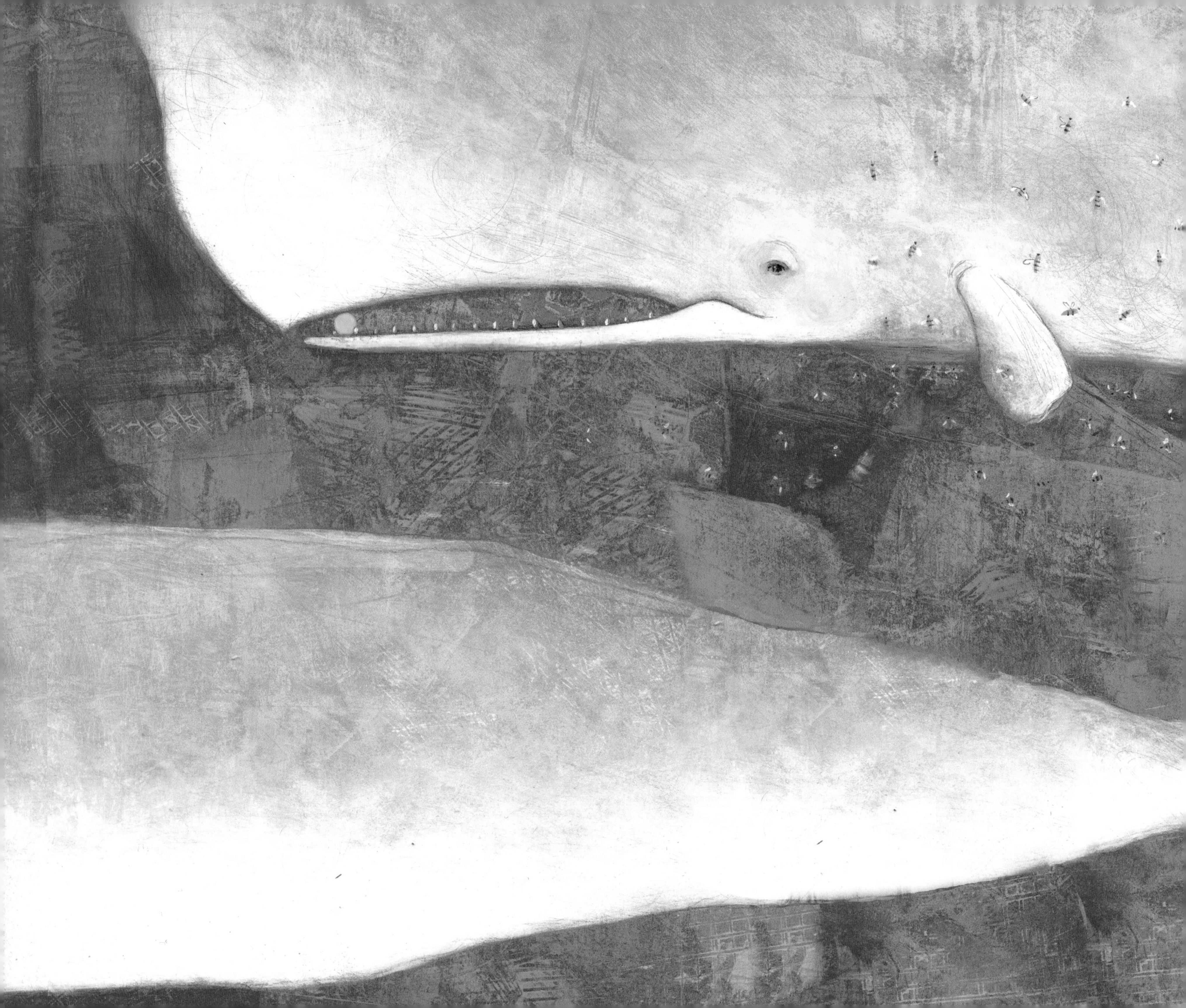

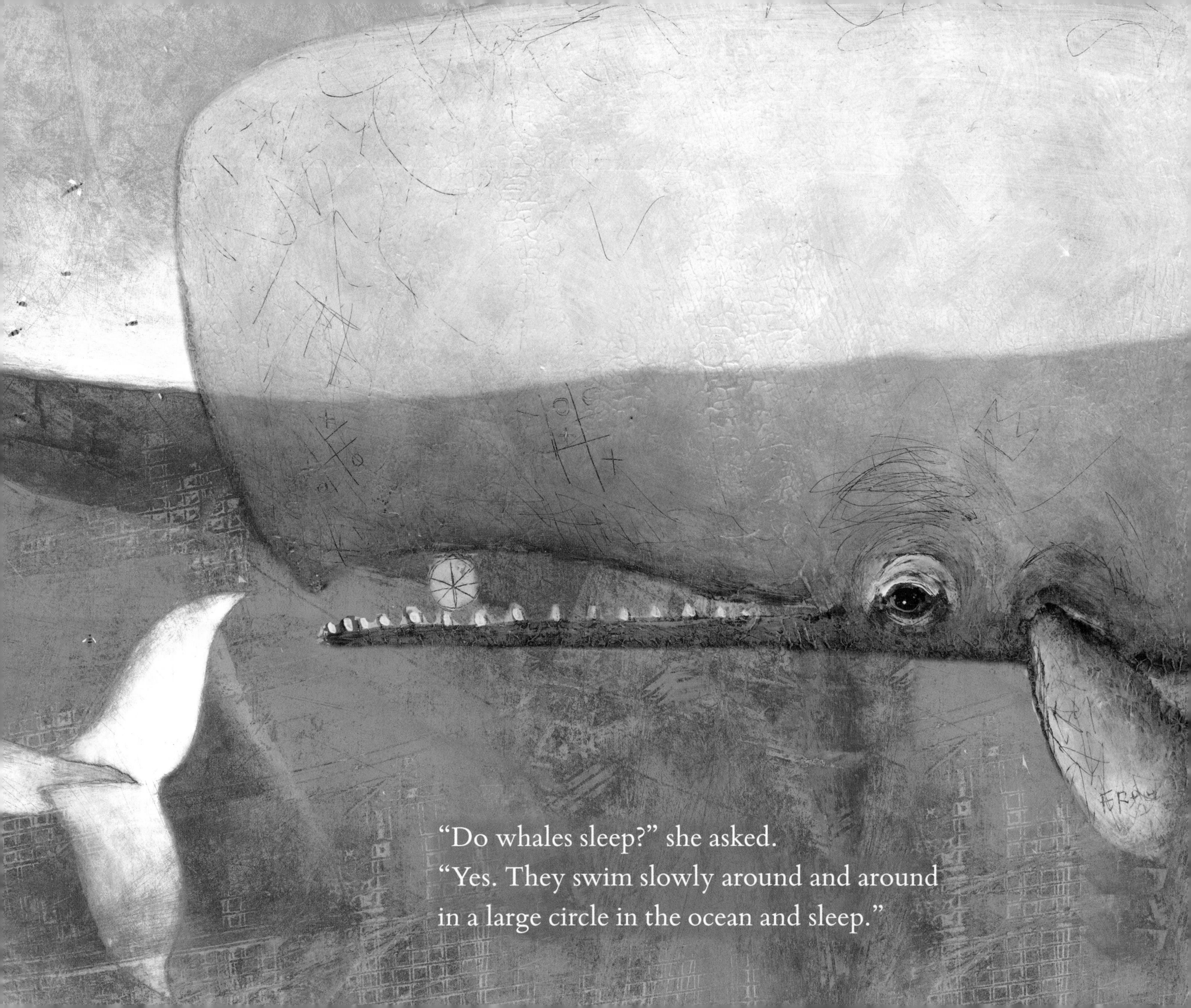

"Do whales sleep?" she asked.
"Yes. They swim slowly around and around
in a large circle in the ocean and sleep."

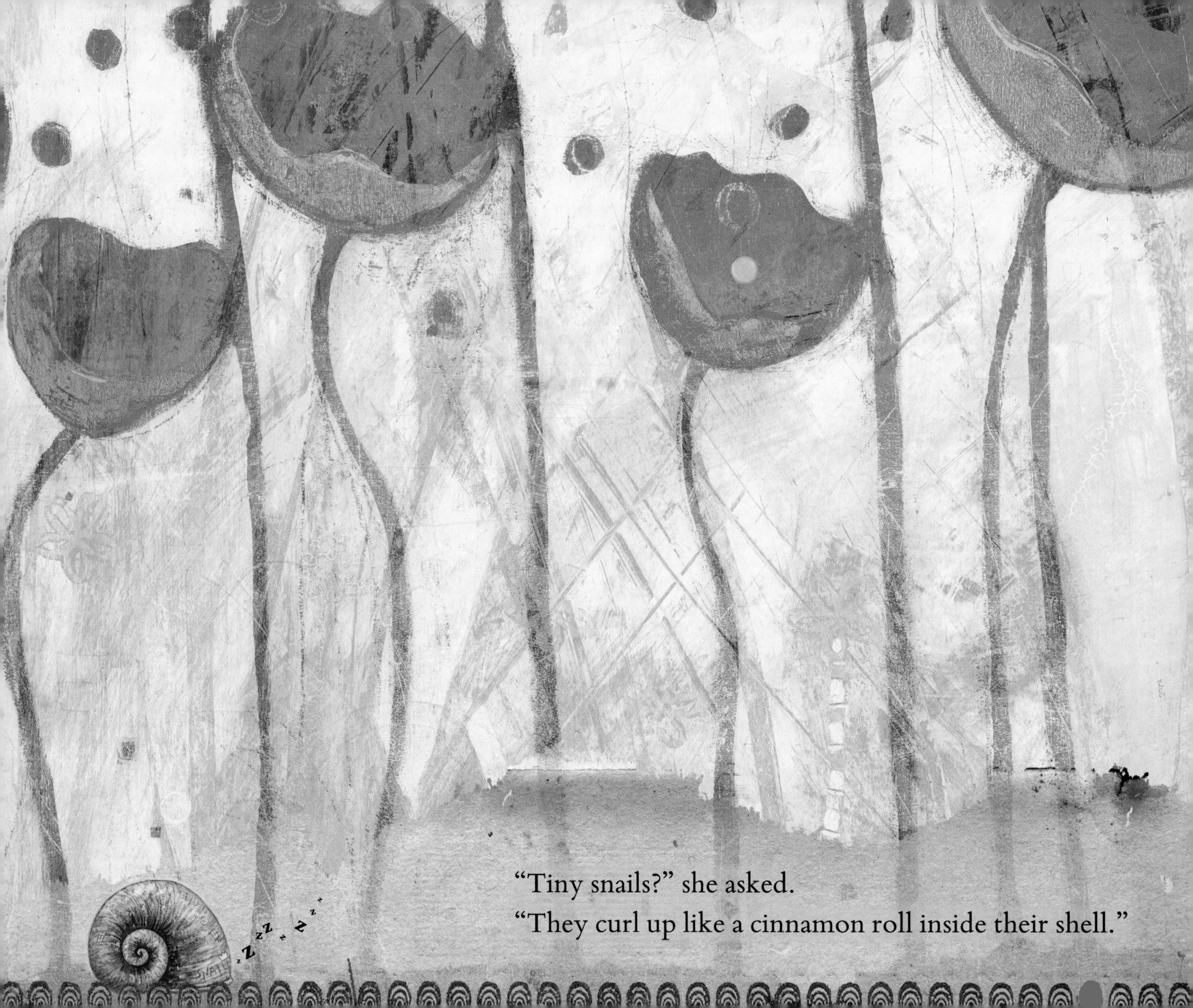

“Tiny snails?” she asked.

“They curl up like a cinnamon roll inside their shell.”

"Even grizzly bears?" she asked.
"Bears are mighty sleepers.
They make a cozy den under the snow
and sleep through the winter."
"All winter! That's too long!" she said.

"Most animals just sleep through the night,"
her parents said, tucking her in.
"I know an animal that sleeps a lot,"
the little girl told them.
"What animal is that?"
her parents asked.

The Little Prince

"The tiger in the jungle.
When he's not hunting, he finds some shade,
closes his eyes, and sleeps.
That way he stays strong."

Her parents nodded. “Sleep is good for that.”
Then they kissed her, turned out the light,
and stood in the doorway.
“I’m still not sleepy,” she told them.
“We know,” they agreed.
“You can stay awake all night long.”
They left her door open a crack.

The little girl's bed was warm
and cozy,
a cocoon of sheets,
a nest of blankets.
Unlike the dog on the couch,
she was right where
she was supposed to be.

She wriggled down under
the covers until she found
the warmest spot,
like the cat in front
of the fire.

She folded her arms
like the wings of a bat.

She circled around like the whale . . .

and the curled-up snail.

Then she snuggled deep
as a bear,
the deep-sleeping bear,

and like the strong tiger, fell fast . . .

asleep.

108